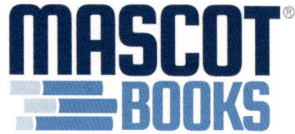

www.mascotbooks.com

Come On, Calm!

©2019 Kelsey Brown. All Rights Reserved. No part of this publication may be reproduced, stored in a retrieval system or transmitted in any form by any means electronic, mechanical, or photocopying, recording or otherwise without the permission of the author.

Second printing. This Mascot Books edition printed in 2021.

For more information, please contact:
Mascot Books
620 Herndon Parkway, Suite 320
Herndon, VA 20170
info@mascotbooks.com

Library of Congress Control Number: 2018912768

CPSIA Code: PRT1021B
ISBN-13: 978-1-64307-247-0

Printed in the United States

But it's okay,
I know what to do!

COME ON, CALM!

I peek in the jungle and what do I find? It's my favorite flower growing on a vine.

I hold the petals gently close to my nose and

SNIFF
SNIFF
SNIFF

with both eyes closed.

COME ON, CALM!

Now in the castle,
friends train to sword fight.

Wearing chainmail and armor,
so they feel all right.

My fingers

PAT PAT

on one arm then the other.

Up and down,

down and up,

they turn over and over.

COME ON, CALM!

On a hot summer day, we drink lemonade.

Lemons, water, and sugar—that's how it's made.

I **SQUEEZE**

with my hands and twist them real tight.

The lemon juice gathers from all of my might.

and put on my coat one arm at a time.

I ZIP up and breathe in frosty air, just enough,

and ZIP down and breathe out, seeing my breath in a puff.

COME ON, CALM!

In the studio, I see the artist make art.

With many colors, he paints from the heart.

I BRUSH BRUSH BRUSH pretend paint on my cheeks.

With my favorite colors,
I draw squiggles and streaks.

COME ON, CALM!

From bubble to bubble,
I twirl and I hop.

I dance and I play,
careful not to pop.

I take a deep breath and

BLOW

out with my lips.

The bubbles fly up and then fall with a dip.

COME ON,
CALM!

I REACH

out my arms to the sky
full of stars,

and touch them, each one,
from real near to real far.

Now for an adventure down by the sea—
the waves rush by and I feel the breeze.

COME ON, CALM!

I WIGGLE my toes down in the sand.

Ten little toes move as fast as they can.

I look in the mirror and what do I see?

The calm I've been looking for is all over me!

A deep breath in from head to toe,

a nice big **HUG,** and I'm ready to go!

ABOUT THE AUTHOR!

Kelsey Brown is a neurodivergent Speech-Language Pathologist, teaching artist, and cultural access advocate. She has a Master's degree in Communication Disorders from Emerson College and Bachelor's degrees in Communication Sciences and Disorders and Theatre from The University of Georgia. Kelsey has always believed in the power of reading and is excited about the magic *Come On, Calm!* brings to its readers.

ABOUT THE ILLUSTRATOR!

Joseph Wrightson is a music educator turned Creative Media Designer & Outreach Coordinator. He has a Bachelor's degree in Music Education from University of Kentucky. Joseph always dreamed about being a children's book illustrator and is thrilled for the next step in this book's journey.

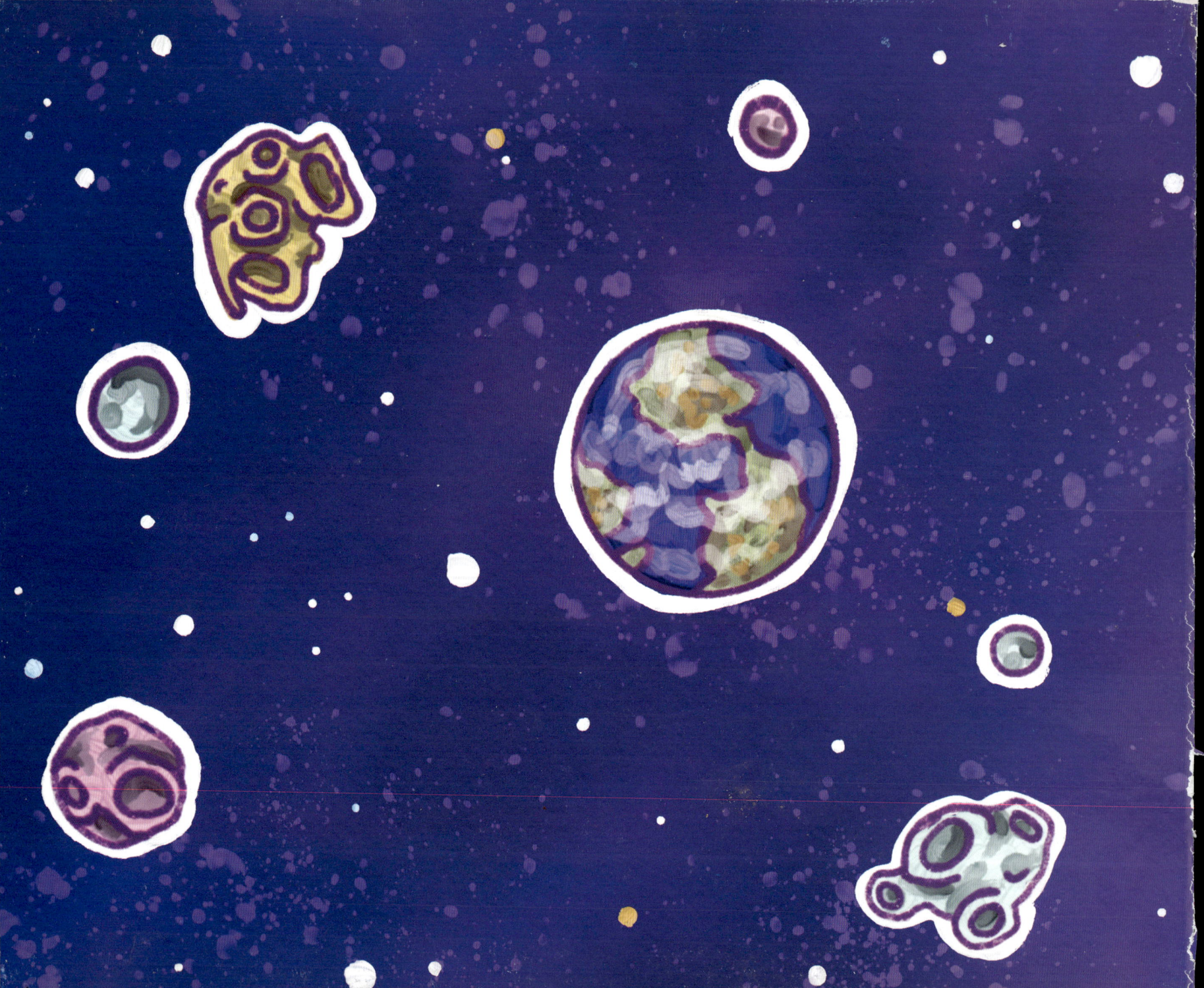